BACKFIELD BLOW

BY JAKE MADDOX

Text by Eric Stevens
Illustrated by Jesus Aburto

STONE ARCH BOOKS
a capstone imprint

Jake Maddox is published by Stone Arch Books, an imprint of Capstone.
1710 Roe Crest Drive, North Mankato, Minnesota 56003
www.capstonepub.com

Library of Congress Cataloging-in-Publication Data is available on the Library of Congress website.
ISBN: 9781663911278 (hardcover)
ISBN: 9781663921864 (paperback)
ISBN: 9781663911247 (ebook PDF)

Summary: Nothing can stop star running back Harris Weathers—until he takes a jarring hit, narrowly escaping injury. Harris is fine, physically, but his nerves are rattled. Does he love football enough to risk a big hit again?

Designer: Bobbie Nuytten

Printed in the United States 5028

TABLE OF CONTENTS

CHAPTER 1

SLAMMED!

Harris Weathers closed his eyes as he listened to Sy Berner call the play numbers. Harris was the star running back for the Tigers and the fastest sixth-grader at Bader Ginsburg Middle School. Sy was his quarterback. Harris pictured in his mind the steps he'd take and the yards he'd gain. He opened his eyes, shook his head, and smiled.

Harris drew back before the snap and ran behind Sy. The center snapped the ball. Sy took it and turned to his right. He slipped the ball against Harris's jersey. Harris slyly pulled the ball into his arms and cut to the left.

Sy stepped back like he would pass. The defensive line swarmed him as Harris took off down the sideline.

Harris was fast, and the Washington Wasps' defense didn't know he had the ball. Harris crossed the thirty-yard line. The end zone was in sight. A touchdown would give the Tigers a win for their first game of the season.

A passing defender took off after Harris as he crossed the twenty-five. This Wasp was fast.

Harris heard his teammates, friends, and family cheering him on. They were loud, calling out, "Go, Harris!" and "Woo-hoo, Weathers!"

Still, over the cheering, he could hear the fast footsteps of the Wasp behind him. Harris was only fifteen yards from the game-winning touchdown. He put on all the speed he had left.

Just as Harris stepped into the end zone, the Wasp caught him. The defender hit him from behind, knocking him to the ground. Harris's head slammed into the turf. All the air was forced from his chest and caught in his throat.

The whistle blew. Harris rolled onto his back and saw the referee standing nearby with both his hands raised—*Touchdown!*

The ref was blurry, though, and Harris struggled to catch his breath. Behind him, Harris could make out his mom and dad, Coach Andersen, and Sy Berner running toward him.

Harris tried to get to his feet to celebrate with them, but he stumbled and fell. He noticed his friends and family weren't smiling like they should have been. They looked worried. Mom looked terrified.

Oh no, Harris thought. I'm hurt.

CHAPTER 2

SHAKEN UP

A bright light shined in Harris's right eye and then his left.

"Harris will be fine," said Dr. Pollie, the school's doctor. She kneeled beside him in the end zone and turned off her penlight. "Looks like no concussion."

"Oh, thank goodness," Harris's mom said.

"How do you feel, Weathers?" asked Coach Andersen.

"Just a little shaken up," Harris said.

"You got the wind knocked out of you," Dr. Pollie said. "You took a pretty good bang to the head, even with the helmet."

"Can I finish the game?" Harris asked.

Coach Andersen shook his head. "You just scored the winning touchdown!" he said. "I think you can sit out the last three seconds of play, don't you?"

"Oh, right," Harris said. "I forgot. It's over."

"Oh, my," Mom said. "Are you sure he's OK, doctor?"

Dr. Pollie stood up and put her penlight in the breast pocket of her white jacket. "He should be fine," she said. "Keep an eye on him. He's just a little shaken up."

"That Washington Middle School player ought to be suspended for the rest of the season," Harris's dad said.

Harris sat up. "I'm fine, Dad," he said. "It's football, right?"

Harris's dad didn't reply. Behind him, Harris saw the Wasp defender with his helmet off, looking on with concern.

"I'm OK, man," Harris called to him. "Solid hit."

"A little late, though," the Wasp replied. "Nice run."

"Thanks," Harris said.

Dad helped Harris to the sideline.

"I'm OK, Dad," Harris said again. "I don't need help walking."

"I know," Mr. Weathers said. "Maybe I just want to walk with my winning-touchdown-scoring, all-star running back son?"

Harris laughed. "Sure, Dad."

*****

On Monday morning, Harris was startled awake early. He'd been dreaming that he was running away from a giant man in football gear. Just as the giant closed in on him, Harris's eye opened. His heart was pounding. The rest of his family was still sleeping.

TIGERS

He grabbed a flashlight and went into the bathroom. He wanted to make sure he was OK. Standing in front of the mirror, he shined the flashlight into his eyes.

The pupils in his eyes—the smallest black part right in the center—shrank from large to very small almost instantly. When he turned off the flashlight, his pupils slowly grew larger again. He knew enough about concussions to know that was a good sign. Dr. Pollie was right.

Harris breathed a sigh of relief. Quietly, he left the bathroom, put the flashlight away, and went back to sleep.

CHAPTER 3

FIFTY PERCENT

When the final bell rang, Harris suited up for practice. After laps, Coach Andersen called the boys in.

"Great job on Friday, Tigers," he said. "O team, set up for drills. D team, follow me for weight training."

That "O" meant offensive players, and the "D" meant defensive players. As the starting running back, Harris was an offensive player. He jogged over to Sy and the rest of the O team.

Sy lightly patted his helmet. "How's the head today?" he asked.

"Fine," Harris said.

It was fine. It didn't hurt at all. But when Sy asked, Harris felt his stomach flip. Just thinking about the hit he took on Friday made him feel like it had just happened. He put his hands on his stomach and turned away from his friend.

"Let's just get started," Harris mumbled.

Sy clapped his hands. "You heard the man, O team," the quarterback said. "Running and blocking drills."

Half the linemen got into position. The other half pulled on red pinnies over their practice uniforms.

"Pattern one," Sy called.

He crouched behind the center and took the snap. Harris ran behind him, planted his foot, took the handoff, and darted past the center. Sy faded back like he was going for a deep pass. Harris ran about ten yards and slowed down.

"OK, nice," Sy called out. "Set up for number two."

The O team went on like that for nearly an hour—running plays, practicing backfield motion, and going over handoffs, laterals, and forward passes.

In these O team drills, there was no contact. Harris had a good time juking in the backfield, dodging between the defenders, and taking or faking handoffs from Sy.

Coach Andersen blew his whistle. "OK, we're going to scrimmage for the rest of our time today," he said. "Count off ones and twos, put on your pinnies . . . you know the drill."

That was usually how they spent the last forty-five minutes of practice. The boys knew to call out the numbers one and two, switching off. They knew that if you said "two," you put on a red pinny.

Sy and Harris ended up on team one.

"I'll coach the red team," Coach said. "Sy, you call your own plays."

Sy and Harris's team huddled up with team one. "OK, boys," Sy said. "We're going to try that outside run we drilled today. I'll handoff to Weathers and fade back like I'm gonna pass, got it?"

The players nodded.

"On two," Sy said. "Let's go!"

Team one lined up. Sy set up behind the center, and Harris set up at the far end of the offensive line, two steps back.

Sy called out the signals. "Hut, one," he barked. "Hut, two."

Harris drew back and cut behind Sy.

"Hut, hut, hut, hut!" Sy cried, and the center snapped the ball from between his legs up into Sy's arms.

Sy turned to his left, slipped the ball to Harris, and drew back out of the pocket. The wide receiver took off up the field, and Sy pretended to pass.

Meanwhile, Harris sprinted along the left sideline. He'd already gained seven yards on the play before the red team realized it.

Suddenly, two passing defenders pulled away from their players to cut Harris's run short. Harris saw the two boys charging toward him. They both looked huge, their red pinnies waving like warning flags. Before they could reach him, Harris cut out of bounds and stopped running.

Harris tossed the ball to Coach Andersen to set up the next play. Coach shot him a disappointed look. Harris hustled back to the team one huddle.

"Why'd you step out?" Sy asked Harris. "You could have had another ten yards on that run, easy."

"Yeah, you're faster than both those guys," said Dan Robbins, the team center.

"We got the first down, didn't we?" Harris pointed out.

Besides, he thought, *no point in risking an injury for a few more yards. Especially in practice.*

"I guess," Sy said. "Let's get some passing in now."

CHAPTER 4

NIGHTMARE

It was a cold February afternoon. Harris crouched at the end of the offensive line. The Tigers were in the Super Bowl. He watched the puffs of vapor from his nose as he breathed hard. He heard Sy's voice call out the play: a wide end run.

Harris stepped back from the line. He cut behind Sy just as the center snapped the ball. Sy turned and put the ball in Harris's open hands.

"Keep your head down," Sy muttered as he handed off the ball.

"What?" Harris replied, but he had to run. He couldn't wait for Sy to respond.

Harris cut up the sideline. Behind him, he heard the stampeding feet of the defensive line for the Wasps, two tons of defenders chasing him down.

But he was fast, the fastest boy on the Tigers. So why weren't his feet working? As hard as he tried, his feet would barely move. It felt as if they were caught in wet cement.

Harris cried out for blockers at his side to keep him safe. But all he saw were more black and yellow jerseys with those wicked Wasp stripes. These defenders were huge! They couldn't be sixth-grade boys. They towered over him like professional football players.

Harris couldn't beat them. They crashed down on him, slamming him to the ground. From behind him, the defensive linemen plowed onto his helpless body.

He got knocked over and banged around, from one defender to the other. His head bounced around like a pinball. The sky twirled. His stomach heaved.

He screamed out and sat up, covered in sweat. His blankets were tangled around his legs. It was just a dream. Actually, it was a nightmare. And it was the most terrifying nightmare Harris had ever had.

CHAPTER 5

SICK

Harris didn't tell anyone about his nightmare. He went to practice and played safe and careful. Then Friday came along.

Their second game of the season was against the Plainfield Harvesters. It was an away game. Harris sat at the back of the bus with Sy and a few other friends from the team.

The other boys were excited. But Harris could only remember the hit he took the week before and the nightmare he'd had the other night.

His skin felt cold, and his stomach was twisted in knots.

"Hey, you OK, Weathers?" Sy asked. "You look sick."

"Yeah, I don't feel good," Harris said.

When the bus pulled up to Plainfield Middle School, Harris was the last kid off the bus.

Coach Andersen stood at the bottom of the bus steps with his clipboard. He clapped Harris on the back, and Harris stumbled.

"Whoa, you OK, Weathers?" Coach asked.

"Yeah, I think so," Harris said. He thought about it again and quickly added, "Actually, I do feel kinda sick."

"Sick how?" Coach asked.

"Like, in my stomach," Harris said. "I think maybe I have food poisoning or the stomach flu or something."

"Think you might throw up?" asked Coach.

"Maybe," Harris said.

"Head to the locker room with the others," Coach Andersen said. "But don't bother putting on your pads. I think you'll sit this one out."

*****

Harris spent the game in the first row of the visiting team's stands with his mom and dad and little sister, Wendy.

Harris watched his friends out on the field. He watched the second string running back, Lew Gordon, run the plays Harris had practiced all week. Lew was an all-around good guy, but he wasn't as fast as Harris. He didn't know the plays as well as Harris did. Sy had to pass more than he usually did. Harris wanted to be out there in Lew's place.

He wanted to give it his all. But his fear of getting hurt was just too much. The fear really did seem to settle right in his stomach. He didn't know if he could conquer it.

Late in the fourth quarter, the Tigers were down by five points. It was third down, and they were within field goal range.

But a field goal wasn't enough to take the lead. Sy called for a run, hoping to get a first down and set the team up for a touchdown.

Harris watched Lew line up in the backfield. He heard Sy bark out the play. Lew cut around behind Sy as the center snapped the ball.

Lew took the handoff, but he didn't make it smooth or sneaky. When Sy dipped out of the pocket like he was going to pass, the defense wasn't fooled at all. They rushed over the line of scrimmage and knocked Lew down for a loss of four yards.

Harris wouldn't have blown the handoff. He would have gotten that first down, he knew it. But as he watched Lew get up, with a tuft of grass stuck in the face mask of his helmet, he knew he couldn't be out there with them. The Tigers didn't score again that game.

CHAPTER 6

FEELING BETTER?

When the Tigers headed into the visitors' locker room, Harris didn't go with them. He just couldn't face the team.

"How are you feeling, sweetie?" his mom asked as he walked with his family to the car.

"Fine," Harris mumbled.

"No more stomachache?" Dad asked.

Harris shook his head. His parents exchanged a glance.

"Let's get ice cream!" Wendy said.

*****

The Weathers family squeezed into a booth at Crazy Custard Cone with their treats.

"You sure you are feeling better?" Mom asked. "You look a little pale."

Harris nodded. With the game behind him and the next game a whole week away, he felt a little better.

Maybe playing football wouldn't be his thing after all. He was fast enough to join track and field instead, and no one got hurt running laps.

From outside the ice cream shop, Harris heard the squeaking and hissing of a bus coming to a stop. He looked out into the evening twilight and saw the Tigers team stepping off the bus.

"Oh no," he said to himself, sinking into the booth. But the moment the door opened, with Sy Berner at the front of the pack, Harris was spotted—and so was his ice cream cone.

The rest of the team went to the counter to order. But Sy, Dan, and Lew came directly over to his booth.

"Feeling better, Weathers?" Sy asked. But his tone wasn't one of concern. He was angry.

"Um, yeah," Harris said. "Much better. Thanks."

"Usually if I feel like I might throw up, I don't want ice cream," Dan said, suspiciously.

Harris shrugged. "It went away," he said.

Sy turned away from the table with a huff. Lew left with him.

"They didn't seem very happy with you," Mom said.

"That's because they know the Tigers would have won with their star running back," Dad pointed out. "But it's not Harris's fault he wasn't feeling well."

Harris slid even deeper into the booth. He wished he could disappear.

"You really *were* feeling sick, right, Harris?" Dad asked.

"Of course," Harris said. "I didn't even bring it up. Coach Andersen did. He said I looked sick. Even Sy said I looked sick."

"But it went away," Dad clarified.

Harris nodded.

"OK then," Dad said. He went back to eating his ice cream. Harris didn't feel like eating any more.

CHAPTER 7

I QUIT

It was almost two in the morning when Harris rolled over and stared at the red numbers of the clock in his room. He hadn't slept at all. All he could think about was the game. He felt awful for missing it, but whenever he imagined playing, all he could think about was getting hurt.

And he couldn't shake the nightmare he'd had. Harris was exhausted, but he was also scared to go to sleep. Quietly, he got out of bed and snuck down to the kitchen. He poured himself a glass of milk and grabbed a granola bar from the cupboard.

Harris sat in the dark kitchen. He stared out the back door into the yard as he sipped his milk. The yard was covered in orange, yellow, and red leaves. In the dark, though, they looked gray.

Suddenly the kitchen light clicked on. Harris shielded his eyes from the light as his dad sat down next to him.

"Can't sleep?" his dad asked.

Harris shook his head.

"Thinking about football?" his dad asked, knowingly.

Harris nodded.

"Wanna talk about it?" he asked.

Harris shrugged.

Mr. Weathers got up and poured himself a glass of milk. He sat down next to Harris again and stole a bite of his granola bar.

“I don’t think I had a stomach flu or food poisoning today,” Harris said.

“No?” his dad said.

“I think I was just nervous,” Harris admitted.

“Nerves can definitely make a person feel sick or like they want to throw up,” his dad said.

“I guess,” Harris said. “The truth is, since I got hit last week, I’ve been a little scared to play. I haven’t been trying very hard in practice. I’ve been stepping out of bounds and dropping the ball before the other guys have a chance to knock into me.”

Mr. Weathers nodded slowly. “I see,” he said. “Well, I can understand that. Mom and I talk all the time about how worried we are having you play a game like football. People get hurt playing football. Head injuries are no joke.”

Harris agreed.

"But people also play football for years and years," Harris's dad went on, "and they get bumps and bruises. But they also love the game, become great team players, and make a lot of great memories."

"Like you did?" Harris asked.

"Yeah," his dad sighed. "Like I did."

Then he looked at Harris and took a deep, slow breath. "But if you want to quit football," he said, "and focus on other things, Mom and I would be OK with that. We want you to be happy *and* safe."

"But that's the thing, Dad," Harris said. "I don't actually want to quit football. I *love* football."

"I know," his dad said.

"I always have," Harris said.

"Ever since I took you to a game when you were only three years old," his dad said.

FLUKES
MILK

His dad gave him a playful elbow to Harris's shoulder. "You thought the players looked like superhero motorcycle riders in their uniforms and helmets."

"I did!" Harris said, laughing.

"And you're great at the game," his dad said. "And you've made good friends. You have been close with Sy Berner for most of your life."

"He's probably my best friend," Harris agreed. He thought back on all of the great plays he and Sy had completed together. He got a rush just thinking about it.

"So, if you don't want to quit," his dad continued, "what do you want to do?"

"I just don't want to be afraid anymore," Harris said.

"Want me to talk to Coach Andersen?" his dad asked.

Harris shook his head. "I will," he said. "First thing Monday."

Dad gave him a side hug. "Good," he said. "Now get some sleep, or you'll be a zombie all weekend."

CHAPTER 8

HEADS UP

On Monday morning before advisory class, Harris knocked on Coach Andersen's office door.

"Come on in, Weathers," Coach said. He didn't get up from his desk. "I think I know what this is about."

"You do?" Harris said as he stepped inside the little office. He sat in the ancient green and gray chair across from the coach. It was probably older than his parents.

"You're quitting football, aren't you?" Coach Andersen said. He shook his head sadly. "You won't be the first player to let fear of the game get the better of him."

"Oh, no, Coach," Harris said. "I mean, I thought about it. But I love football too much to quit. But how did you know . . . I mean, I *have* been scared lately."

Coach Andersen stood up and looked out the window at the school's football field. "I've seen you in practice," Coach said. "Ever since you took that hit at the game against Washington, you've been playing fifty percent. Your heart's not in it."

"I'm . . . I'm sorry," was all Harris could think to say.

Coach Andersen shook his head and turned to look at Harris. "Nothing to be sorry about," he said. "It's my job as coach to make sure you're not only playing with all your heart, but staying safe while you do it. That's why I got these for the whole team." Coach pulled a box out from under his desk. "They arrived this weekend."

He opened the box and pulled out a funny looking black beanie. "You wear it under your helmet. It lessens the shock to your head when you take a hit," he explained.

He tossed it to Harris.

Harris inspected the beanie, squishing the gel inserts between his fingers.

"That hit you took," Coach Andersen said, "and your nervous stomach on Friday afternoon were a wake-up call to me and the athletic board."

"Wow, really?" Harris said.

"Yep. A few of the board members were watching. We decided we should try to prevent head injuries before something serious happens," Coach Andersen said. "That means better equipment, like these beanies, and more focus in practice on preventing injuries."

"That really makes me feel better, Coach," Harris said. "Thanks."

"It makes *me* feel better that you don't want to quit," Coach replied. "Thanks for coming to talk to me."

Harris smiled. A sense of calm settled over him that he hadn't felt in awhile.

Suddenly, the bell rang.

"You're a good kid, Weathers," Coach said. "Now get to class."

*****

At practice, Coach Andersen gathered everyone around. He passed out the gel beanies and explained what they were for. Everyone put one on under their helmet.

"O team, get set up for drills," he said. "Sy's in charge."

"Put your hearts into it out there," he said, nodding at Harris.

Harris stood next to Sy. "We good?" Harris asked quietly.

"Yeah, it's cool," Sy said. But Harris wasn't entirely convinced Sy meant it.

"D team," Coach Andersen continued, "we're working on heads-up play today. Can anyone tell me what that means?"

Dan raised his hand. "That means tackling without ramming headfirst, right?" he said.

"That's right," Coach Andersen said. "Today's all about safety, and that has to start with tackles. Especially you big guys. You know you could put a scrawny kicker in the hospital, and we don't want that."

The big guys on the D team laughed.

But Coach Andersen cut them off. "This is no joke, boys. Think how you'd feel if you ended a fellow player's football career before it really got started. And that's not to mention something more serious that might affect a person's whole life."

The laughing stopped.

"Let's get started," Coach Andersen said.

*****

"Ready?" Sy asked Harris as they lined up.

Harris thumped his helmet with his fist. "Yup," he said. "Pattern one: backfield switch."

Sy nodded and took his place behind the center. Harris stood at the left end of the offensive line.

Sy started the count. Harris drew back and cut behind Sy, but then he switched direction.

Sy took the snap, and Harris faded toward the sideline. Sy fell back out of the pocket as the defenders closed in on him. He pulled back for a long pass—but threw a short one to Harris just over the line of scrimmage near the boundary line.

Harris snatched the ball out of the air and tucked it under his arm. He sprinted up the sideline.

Two passing defenders moved toward him, and he nearly stepped out to avoid them. But then he remembered the extra gel under his helmet, and he remembered that he loved this game.

Harris sped toward the defenders and spun, leaving one in the dust. The other got a hold of his middle and brought him to the ground. Both boys fell to the turf.

Harris nearly laughed with relief. The tackle hadn't even hurt.

"Nice run," said the tackler. "Welcome back."

"Thanks," Harris said. "Good to be back!"

CHAPTER 9

THE RIVALRY

On Friday afternoon, the Mount Meadow Marlins played at the Tigers. In the locker room before the game, Coach Andersen paced in front of the team. "As you know," he said, "we play the Marlins once every year."

He stopped pacing and stared at each player as he spoke. "As you also know," he went on, "the Marlins have beaten the Tigers every year for the past nine years."

He sighed. "That first time they won was also my first year coaching at Bader Ginsburg Middle School. And it was the first year my college roommate, Dean Finch, became the head coach at Mount Meadow Middle School."

The team winced.

"Our ten-year reunion will be this spring," Coach said as he resumed pacing. "No pressure . . . but I don't intend to go into that event hall with a 0–10 record against my old friend."

"We won't let you down, Coach," Sy said.

"Ready to start today, Weathers?" Coach asked.

"Definitely," Harris replied. "I'll play with all my heart."

Coach Andersen nodded. "Get out there, Tigers! Leave it all on the field!"

*****

After the kickoff, the Tigers had possession at their forty-two-yard line. Sy called a lateral to the halfback. Harris set up at the end of the offensive line. Sy got the snap and took two steps back.

He pitched the ball to Mateo, behind Harris. Harris ran with Mateo up the middle of the field. He pushed off a defender, giving Mateo a little more open field. The halfback got to the fifty before the Marlins' defense brought him down.

Sy brought in the huddle. "I'm going to Mateo again," he said. "This time step up and turn for the quick pass. Pattern three."

"Hey," Harris said. "Don't forget about me."

"I haven't," Sy said. "Break."

The team lined up. Sy took the snap and faded three steps back. Harris ran around behind him for the fake handoff. He sprinted upfield along the sideline, bringing three defenders with him.

Sy fired a line-drive spiral into Mateo's chest. He made the catch, but the Marlins didn't let him take a step. It was a gain of one yard.

"Third down," Sy said in the huddle. "Paulie, pass to you ten yards out, button hook. Be ready."

"Sy," Harris said.

Sy ignored him. "Break!"

Harris lined up behind the offensive line. Paulie, a receiver, stood behind him.

Sy took the snap. Harris and Paulie pushed through the line, with their linemen clearing a path. Paulie went out ten yards and spun back to catch Sy's pass, but a defender jumped and knocked the ball away.

It was fourth down, with three yards to go.

"Come on out, boys," Coach Andersen said. "Special teams."

They were punting, and Harris didn't even have a chance to get the first down.

"Sy, you don't have to worry about me," Harris said as they walked to the bench. "I'm not going to throw the game. I'm fine now."

"I know," Sy said. "Don't worry about it."

Harris watched the kicking team set up and lay a nice punt inside the Marlins' twenty-yard-line.

They ran it back to the thirty. They got the first down twice, but then only got as far as the Tigers' twenty-five. It was close enough for the field goal.

The Marlins were up 3–0.

CHAPTER 10

HAVE HEART

Harris took a few runs, but Sy didn't rely on him for yardage as much as he usually did. By the end of the fourth quarter, Harris had run for fifty yards. Sy had passed for a hundred and fifty. And the Tigers were down 13–9.

After a Marlins kickoff, Coach Andersen called a time-out.

"This game is far from over," Coach said. "One touchdown, and we win. That's when it's over."

"We just can't get into that end zone," Sy said. "Their passing defense is strong."

"Give it to Harris," Coach said. "Let him take the end run. He'll get it there. Isn't that right, Weathers?"

"I'll give it everything I have," Harris said, glancing at Sy. "I can promise that."

Sy exhaled through his nose sharply. "Fine," he said. "Pattern one. Get us that first down, Harris."

The O team took the field and lined up. Sy counted off. Harris stepped back from the line and darted across the backfield. Sy took the snap, spun to his left, and slipped the ball into Harris's hands. Harris shot upfield. Sy faded back and went to pass. But he didn't have the ball. Harris did.

Harris weaved through the defense. He spun past a corner back. Paulie's defender broke off from the receiver. He chased after Harris. Harris saw him coming from the edge of his vision. He was big.

Harris's breath caught as he remembered his nightmare: towering defenders and bone-splintering slams. His head bouncing against the turf. His whole world spinning.

Harris took a deep breath as the Marlins defender knocked into him with his shoulder. They both went to the ground out of bounds.

"First down!" the line ref called out.

Harris jogged back to the huddle.

"You good, Weathers?" Sy asked.

Harris nodded. "Yeah," he said. "Touch and go for a minute, but I'm good."

"OK," Sy said. "Pattern one, backfield switch. Left side. Break!"

The O team lined up. Harris drew back on the left side. He breathed slowly. He imagined the ball in his hands. He remembered heads-up. He remembered the gel padding under his helmet.

Sy called *hut*. Harris left the line and jogged behind Sy. Sy took the snap. Harris cut backward, passing behind Sy again, and went out wide to the left in the backfield. Sy drew back for the long pass, but he found Harris instead with the lateral.

Harris snagged the ball from the air and pulled it against him. The defensive line swarmed in on Sy too late. Mateo ran alongside Harris. He blocked two defenders then tumbled to the turf.

Harris sprinted on alone. Several Marlins tried to catch him. One dove for his feet but missed. Harris crossed the forty, the thirty-five, the thirty-yard line.

One Marlin went to cut him off from the end zone. His head up, Harris ran toward the defender. He spun out away from the sideline. The Marlin tripped up, dove, and missed the tackle.

Harris stepped over the end zone line for the touchdown. He dropped the ball and jumped, his hands in the air. In a moment, the rest of the O team ran into the end zone too. They grabbed him and raised him up on their shoulders.

The Tigers had finally beaten the Marlins.

"Great run, Harris," Sy said.

Harris's teammates let him down from their shoulders. He and Sy jogged back to the bench. Only a few seconds were left on the clock. The game was over.

"Thanks for trusting me," Harris said.

"Thanks for showing up," Sy said. He patted Harris on the helmet.

Sy grabbed some water. Harris sat on the bench.

"Nice job, Weathers," Coach Andersen said. "How's the padding? Feel OK?"

“Feels great, Coach,” Harris said. “It’s not just protecting my head, though.”

“What do you mean?” Coach asked.

“It’s protecting my heart too,” Harris said. “And if I can play with heart, I can give it my all and that’s what really matters.”

AUTHOR BIO

Eric Stevens has written more than one hundred chapter books for young readers. He lives with his wife and children in Minneapolis, where he and his family enjoy kayaking, cycling, and playing tennis in the city's beautiful parks.

ILLUSTRATOR BIO

Jesus Aburto has worked in the comic book industry for more than eleven years. In that time, he has illustrated popular characters such as Wolverine, Iron Man, Blade, and the Punisher. Recently, Jesus started his own illustration studio called Graphikslava. He lives in Monterrey, Mexico, with his kids Ilka, Mila, Aleph, and his beloved wife.

GLOSSARY

backfield (BACK-feeld)—the area behind either the offensive or defensive line

concussion (kuhn-KUH-shuhn)—an injury to the brain caused by a hard blow to the head

contact (KAHN-takt)—touching something

juke (JOOK)—to make a quick move to fake out an opponent

lateral (LAT-ur-uhl)—to pass the ball sideways or backward to another player

pinny (PIN-ee)—loose shirts often worn in practice games

pocket (POK-it)—the area behind the offensive line from which a quarterback usually throws passes

scrimmage (SKRIM-ij)—a practice game

turf (TURF)—the surface layer of grass and earth on a lawn or playing field

DISCUSSION QUESTIONS

1. Why did Harris Weathers play so carefully after he took a painful hit in the first game?

2. Harris complained of a stomachache in chapter five. Did he have food poisoning or a stomach bug, or did something else cause his stomach pain? Explain.

3. Why was Sy angry to see Harris at the ice cream shop after the game?

WRITING PROMPTS

1. Have you ever been hurt while taking part in a sport? Were you able to go back to the sport? How did you handle it?

2. If Harris were a friend of yours, what would you say to him? How would you help him get past his fear and back to the sport he loved in a safe way?

3. Have you ever given up on something, like a sport, a craft, or some other activity because it got to be too difficult? Looking back, do you wish you had stuck with it? Why or why not?

MORE ABOUT HEAD INJURIES AND SPORTS

Kids ages 9 to 14 make up the largest group of football players in the United States. Luckily, kids that age also tend to knock into each other during play a lot less roughly than older, bigger players. For that reason, head injuries among young players are uncommon.

However, young players also have weaker necks, larger heads, and less natural protection around their brains. So when a big hit does occur in play, an injury may be more likely.

Experts say it's important to do everything possible to prevent injuries from happening. Review the following tips to stay safe.

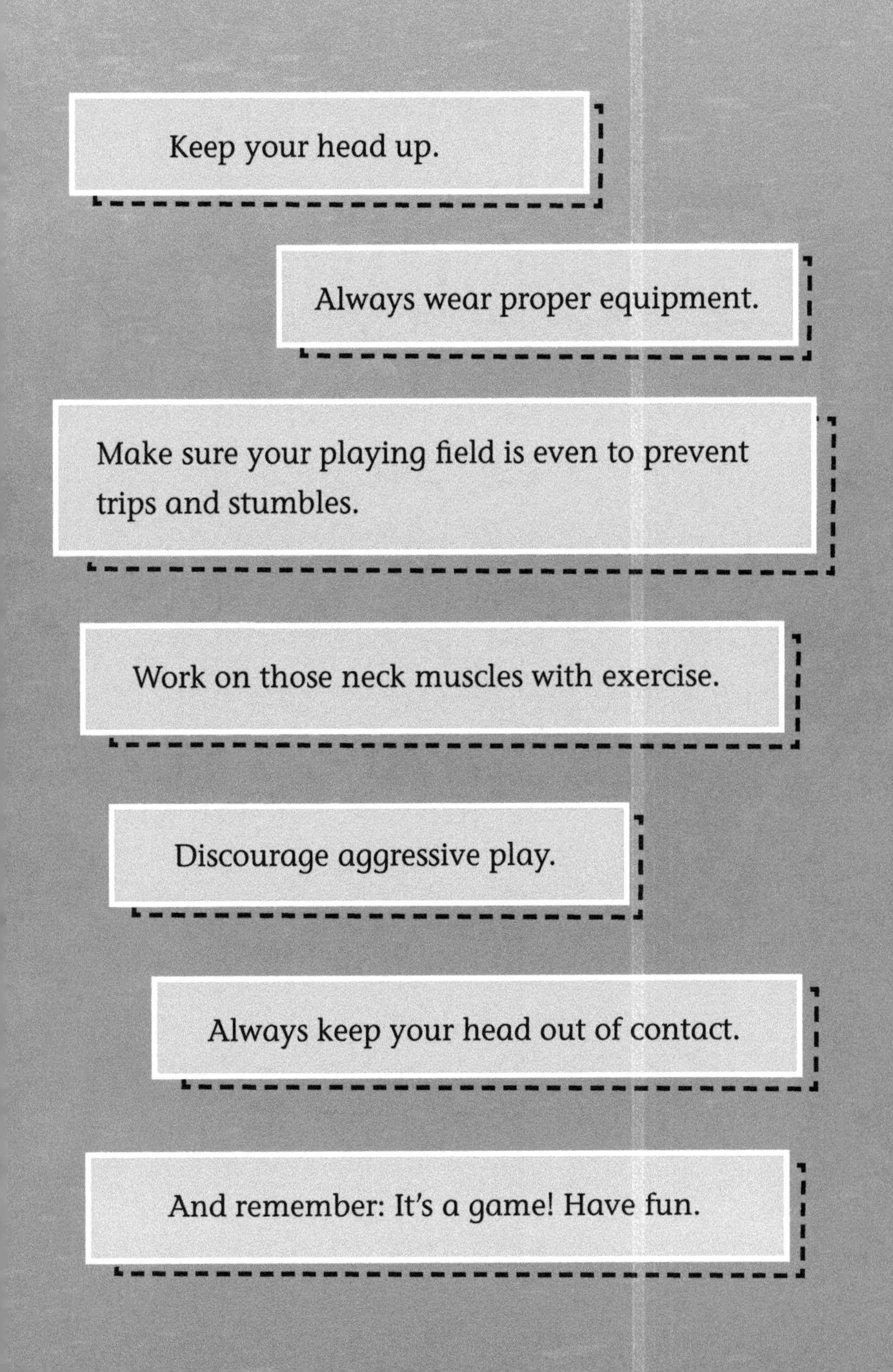
Keep your head up.

Always wear proper equipment.

Make sure your playing field is even to prevent trips and stumbles.

Work on those neck muscles with exercise.

Discourage aggressive play.

Always keep your head out of contact.

And remember: It's a game! Have fun.

MORE FROM JAKE MADDOX!

- BLUE LINE BREAKAWAY
- PICK AND ROLL
- DIAMOND DOUBLE PLAY
- UNDERCOVER BMX

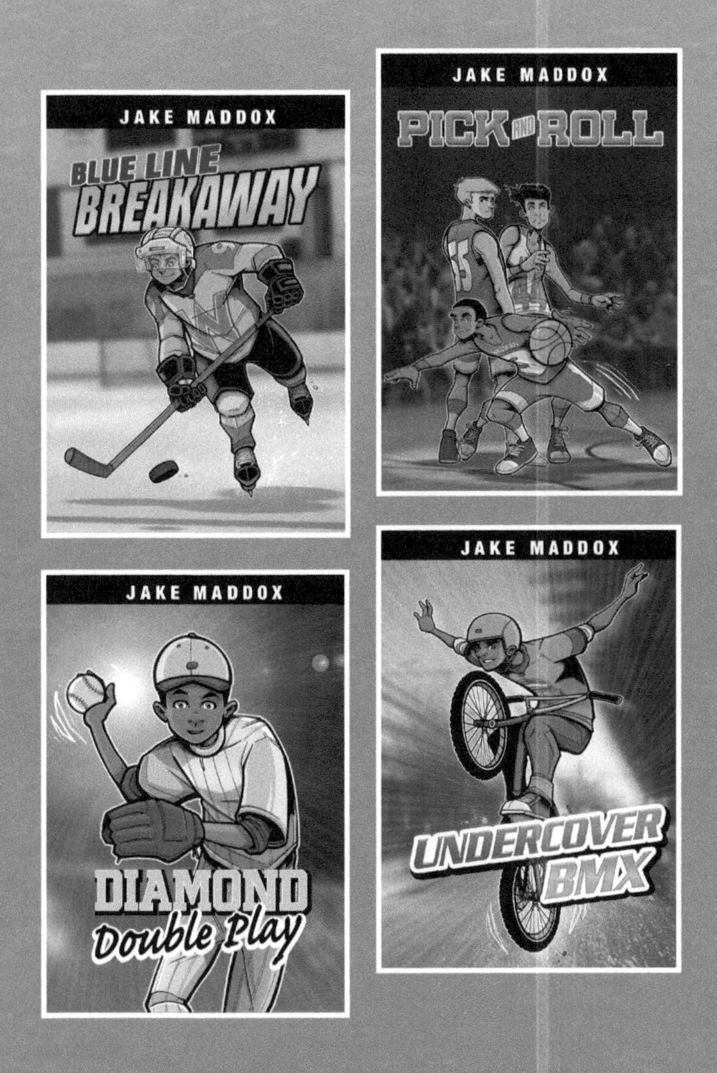

READ THEM ALL !